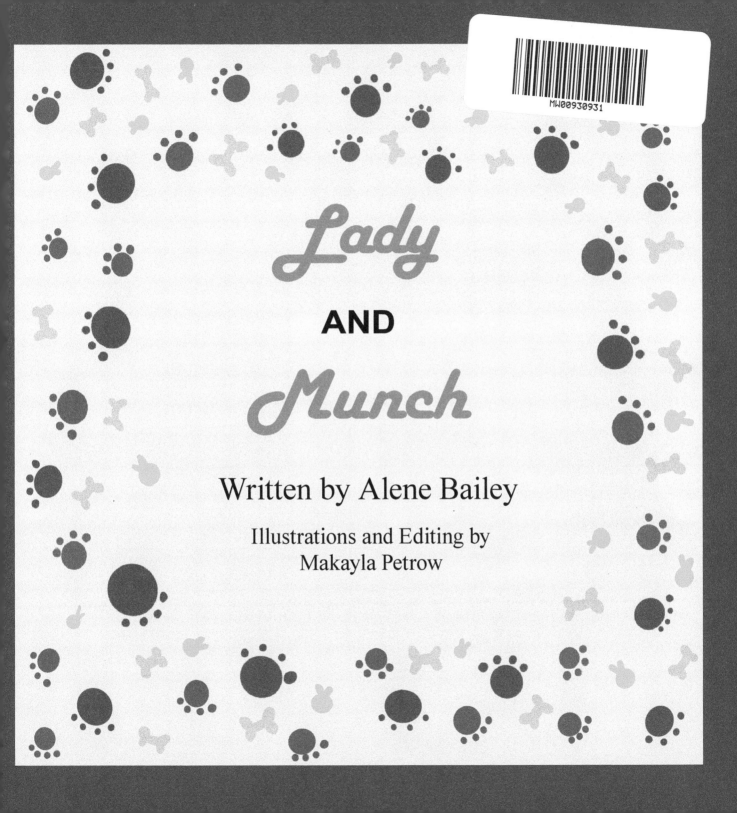

Lady

AND

Munch

Written by Alene Bailey

Illustrations and Editing by
Makayla Petrow

Lady

AND

Munch

Written by Alene Bailey

**Illustrations and Editing by
Makayla Petrow**

© 2021 Alene Bailey

ISBN 978-0-9861530-4-4

Nation of Publication:
United States

Published by:
Fox Publications, LLC
Flagstaff, Arizona, 86005

Dedication

Lady and Munch dedicate this book to all our furry friends and their beloved owners.

This book belongs to:

_____

Hello, this is Lady.

Lady was

born on a warm

June day.

She lives

with

Grandma

and

Grandpa

B.

Lady loved to catch a throwing disk...

...and fetch a ball.

3

One day
Lady sat in
the window
watching
Grandma
and
Grandpa B
cook
outside on
the grill.

Being alone made her sad. She would
do anything to be next to them.

As Grandma B brought the food inside, Lady

dashed towards the door and crashed right into her.

Food flew through the air!

Crack! went Grandma B's foot.

"Laaady!" she yelled, as the puppy ran around the yard.

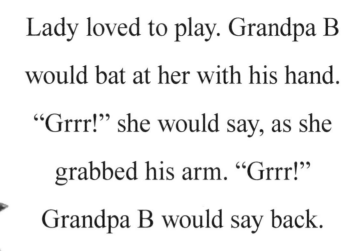

Lady loved to play. Grandpa B would bat at her with his hand. "Grrr!" she would say, as she grabbed his arm. "Grrr!" Grandpa B would say back.

After playing, Grandpa B would sit in his rocking chair with Lady at his feet. "Daddy's baby," he would say to her. "Daddy's baby."

They would go for rides in Grandpa B's truck.

"Come on, Lady! Wanna go for a ride?"

Lady loved going for rides. She would sit in the passenger seat and hang her head out of the window.

Bbrr

One time, Grandma B wanted to come with them.
She opened the passenger door to see
Lady sitting right in her seat! "Move over,
Lady," Grandma B said, "Move!" Lady wouldn't
move over. Grandma B laughed so hard she
couldn't get into the truck.

Early one morning, Grandma B and Lady saw
a mommy and baby deer lying in the yard.

Everyone was startled as
the mommy deer lunged
towards them and ran back
into the woods.

The days started to turn cool. Grandma and Grandpa B began to bring firewood inside for the winter.

Lady would sit in the front room window and
watch the birds go by. She dreamed of how
nice it would be to have an animal friend.

One chilly night, while lying in front
of the fireplace,

Lady heard a noise.

Suddenly, she ran to the window and moved the curtain over with her nose. Grandma and Grandpa B were surprised to see a fluffy little kitten outside on the window sill!

Grandma B brought the kitten inside.

He was so small that he fit right inside

Grandpa B's palm!

They decided to call him "Munch."

Lady was so excited when Grandpa B set Munch down on the floor. Her tail wagged back and forth.

"Gentle," Grandpa B said, as she rubbed Munch with her nose.

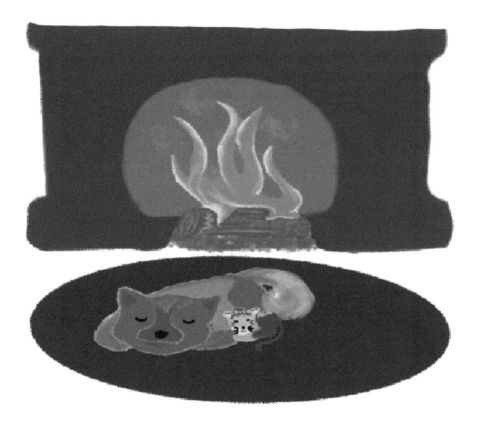

After saying "Hello," they snuggled in front of the fireplace and fell asleep.

The next morning, Munch explored the
house room-by-room.

Lady followed Munch everywhere;

sniffing and nuzzling him with her nose.

They bounced around the house

playing with toys...

...and a pen light.

Back and forth they went.

When they got tired, Munch would sleep in the chair
with Lady at his feet.

Sometimes Munch would bat at Lady with his paw. Lady didn't like that.

One time Munch ran right up behind Lady and smacked her with his paw. Lady turned around and Wham! She hit Munch back and he went rolling across the floor!

Grandma and Grandpa B came home one day and couldn't find Munch anywhere. They called for him, "Munch, Munch...where are you?"

Suddenly, they heard a very soft, "meow...meow!"

"Lady," Grandpa B said, "find Munch!"

"Meow...Meow." Lady followed the muffled sound into the kitchen and looked up at the cabinets. Munch was stuck!

So, up the ladder Grandpa B went and carried Munch down to Grandma B.

It was just about Christmastime and Grandma B
brought home a fresh evergreen tree.

Lady and
Munch
watched her
string up
the lights.

When it was done, they snuggled together

underneath the tree.

A small round ornament with
a bell inside, hung from the
bottom branch of the tree.
Munch knocked it off.
Ring, Ring, Ring!
The ornament jingled as it
rolled across the floor.
"Arf! Arf!" Lady said excitedly.

Curiosity got the best of Munch as he climbed

up the tree. "Ruff, Ruff!" Lady barked.

"Meow, Meow, Meow," Munch responded softly.

Lady and Munch liked Christmas. They would sniff and hit the boxes under the tree. Lady couldn't resist; she ripped the paper off of two presents!

Out popped a small ball and a chew bone.
Somehow, Lady knew those presents were
for her and Munch! They played together
with their new toys.

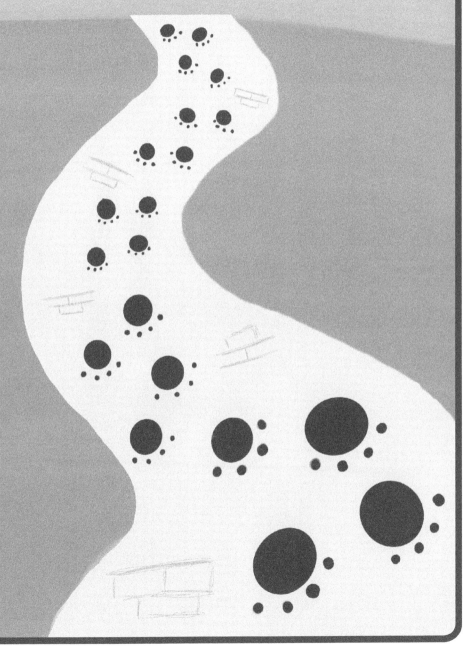

The End

CPSIA information can be obtained
at www.ICGtesting.com
Printed in the USA
BVHW021740120821
614294BV00014B/203